SYLVIE GINESTET

SHADOW PLAY

Dark fantasy novella

Previously published by this author

The Quest – The Imhumvamps V1   February 2014

Publications available in French

Le Miracle – Les Imhumvamps T1   September 2012
La Recouvrance – Les Imhumvamps T2   August 2014
Une vie pour la vie – Les Imhumvamps T   October 2015
Les ombres s'amusent   February 2015

© Illustration and cover: Sylvie Ginestet 2015
All rights reserved.

ISBN: 978-2-9601524-8-7
Formal deposit: D/2015/Ginestet Sylvie, Publisher

First published in French under the title "Les ombres s'amusent' 2015.
Translated from French by "Intuitive Translations", Torquay, United Kingdom.

SYLVIE GINESTET

SHADOW PLAY

Dark fantasy novella

Thanks to Graham for his help to translate this novella from French to English.

Hello, my name is Louie, with an E; a little bit of vanity from my parents, but it has its charm with the girls. I'm twenty-eight years old. The best age you might say!

Two years ago, I was driving on the highway leading to Namur, riding my Harley. I felt invincible, handsome and alive.

The truck was driving too, but a lot faster than me. Maybe he didn't see me... though so big. So, I slid first beneath its grille, and it started to slow down, I saw its trailer veer to the right. I thought it freed us, my Harley and me. I let go and the wheels of his vehicle tossed me from left to right and vice versa. I'm not able today to tell you how long it lasted, but I'm still here.

Hello, my name is Louie, I now ride a chair adapted for my needs. I'm the resident, perhaps lifelong, of this house for life and rehabilitation because I believed I was invincible, but I was just invisible.

My life has changed; I see things from a different angle, and I need another person for most of my daily activities, but I don't lose hope that again one day I can slip onto another different kind of two wheels. The road will be long, but I keep smiling; I have all my time.

My life can be summed up like this; in the morning is the time for care, endurance and suffering. In the afternoon when it's quiet, I glide through the maze of corridors of this institution to explore the basement. Why? I do not know; I'm irresistibly drawn underground.

When evening comes, they move my comrades and me into the communal TV room. There, I can say that I have been lucky; some have encountered much bigger obstacles than I.

My parents and my ex-girlfriend, because I released her from that constraint, visit me every Sunday when the weather is looking good. On that day, no care, no crying; just happiness to see them. Often, they take me far away from this place, and I start to dream that my life could have been different, but that was without counting on this truck full of beer which hit me on another Sunday on the A411. I had never heard of cervical C3, 5 or the rest. Now I can't feel them, so we'll stop talking about them.

I'm neither angry towards the driver nor with destiny, that's the way it had to happen. All I have to do is to review my plans, alter them, and everything will be fine.

Often on Thursday lunchtimes, they serve us potatoes in all kinds of sauces; I love sauces. My caregiver Henri does so a little less, because I'm still struggling to find the way to my mouth without getting it everywhere. He also doesn't lose hope that things will work out.

Doctors and physiotherapists say I'm doing very well; a long rehabilitation of course, but afterwards perhaps some independence could be found.

For a year now, I've been exploring the basement; just to let you know how big it is there. They store so much, there are so many doors to push. That said, I haven't yet found any corpses or torture chambers. Those, they have put on the first floor. I visit them every day almost.

Today it's raining.

At noon, we have French fries. They represent for me a good exercise of manipulation and precision. First, I have to catch one with my fingers; it is, I must admit, the most delicate part, then I dip it in mayonnaise. Henri always puts too much mayonnaise on my plate; it's easier for me. After that it's simple to find the way to my mouth. I've become good at this game. I'm better able to move my arms horizontally than vertically, but I am making progress.

While my friends watch TV on this rainy afternoon, I decide to go exploring. Henri put my Harley cap on me, one that my parents bought me so that I'd never forget how handsome I was.

My wheelchair is electric, but I can disable this function and use it conventionally, with the strength of my arms. I have to develop my muscles if I want to move forward!

Lift three of the west wing; the doors close behind me, I press the "SS 1" button for the first basement, because there are two. Slowly it descends; I can't feel the vibrations in my spine so I press my hand to the wall and close my eyes. A few seconds suffice for me to find myself in an all-white hallway. I have no other choice but to go ahead. There is no door, just the wall of blinding white, but a few turns of my wheels further on, an intersection. I can't decide between the corridor to the right, or to the left; I opt for the left, for ease I admit, having more motivity with my right arm. The corridor is long, very long; a dozen doors on each side. I'm hoping they won't be locked; I don't like this kind of failure. Being stuck behind a closed door is frustrating.

There is no sound.

I roll myself along to the first door, and I stop. I take off my protective glove and operate the handle. It opens. The light switch is within my reach, what luck! Before me, I find a long row of shelves at many levels, needless to say that I can forget about the highest ones. Here there are towels; hundreds, maybe even thousands. Next there are sheets, the majority white; I do however notice some pink and blue ones, perhaps for children. Mine are always white. I can't turn around in the closet, so I go out backwards into the hallway.

I don't know what I'm looking for here; maybe just a little calmness, some solitude, to cry tearlessly over a fate I never wished for myself. Life is full of surprises, not always the best ones. It puts us to the test. I, however, had a different future.

After a good deal of effort, I'm back in the white hallway; I head towards the second door. This time it's situated on the other side of the wall to my right. It's strange; the doors have no lock. I open it with ease, it contains all kinds of household products. If, one day, I get tired of my condition and want to kill myself, I could go and get a towel from the first room and then come here, spray it with a good mixture of ammonia and other things, and so end it once and for all, with no ill effects.

I shut the door, somewhat disappointed.

After several hours and no discovery in the palm of my hand which might allow me to blackmail this exemplary institution, I go back to the dining hall with my fellow patients. Dinner is about to be served; since we have free time in the afternoon, so we must be punctual for dinner. They do a head count of us, help us, and love us for who we are.

"This is a joke!" I exclaimed, when I saw the starter coming.

Soup!

Henri courteously replies.

"You have to try it, come on."

"Put yourself in my place, eh!"

He raises his eyebrows; this isn't the first time he's been told that. He doesn't answer me, and dresses me in a horrible bib for children. My dignity takes a hit, but this isn't the first time for that either.

The meal torture is finally over and has exhausted me, I set my chair up in the fourth row in the television room, and I decide to become lost in the night's film. Fifteen minutes later, a hand is placed on my shoulder, I turn my head as best I can; my Scrabble accomplice gives me a sign inviting me to follow him. With great difficulty, I extricate myself from the audience for the second part of this film, and I join him at the games table.

Pascal is his name, and he's in the same condition as me; sitting in a wheelchair following an accident. The only difference between us, being that he caused the accident. He wanted to die, dragging down an innocent person in his fall. His mind is now forever tormented by his gesture, devoid of meaning. He feels a deathly guilt... I lost tonight, unable to compete with all his morbid words. One day I'll bring him into the depths, to visit the second basement.

All day it's been raining, bringing an anticipated freshness, but now the weather has become stormy and it's too hot to get to sleep. I press the supervisor's doorbell. A young woman in a blue blouse comes, she smiles sweetly to me.

"Hello Louie. What's the matter?"

"Can you help me?" I reply, pointing to my chair.

"Where you do you want to go in the middle of the night?"

"I can't sleep, I'll go and stroll about a bit."

"Okay," she replies, coming over and pushing my chair.

Nobody remarks on my somewhat misplaced humor. One day, a psychologist told me that this helps me to accept everything.

"Thank you, Louise."

Just a coincidence, believe me.

At night, there's no one in the corridors. They all go back to their rooms to dream a little, and to no longer feel the weight of their troubles. I hear sometimes, amongst the snoring, the cries of those who endlessly relive the events that led them here.

I head over to the elevator; the button "SS2" is calling me.

I'm not done with my first attempt with the "SS2", I think I've explored a good half. At this level, the walls are grey, not dirty; no. This is a chosen color, a color which was unanimously passed by the administration board! I don't tarry in the part which I know, and therefore I'm pushed into the pervading greyness, trying to remember where I left off last time.

It's not only the color that changes here, the doors are also different. They're thicker; some I have a problem with opening, or even just pushing, they're so heavy. Now I stop, here facing a new door: blue... this time!

I don't understand why they painted it that color. This drives my curiosity and excitement to a peak. I take my gloves off, hoping that the light won't go out, and get ready to turn the handle (everything is different on this floor, I told you). It opens wide, as if it could do nothing else but be either fully closed or fully open. It invites me to enter. I don't know whether opening it automatically activated the light, but it's daylight inside. Not artificial fluorescent light, but a kind of natural light, despite the lack of a window. I enter within and the door closes on its own behind me.

"Clack".

Here I am, shut in an empty room. I wonder how it can serve them. Wherever I look, there's only nothingness. The walls are all white except for one. A large picture has been placed there, covering the entire area of the wall. This depicts a full field of wild flowers. I'm dreaming, I think.

I approach gently, and place my hand on the wall; it would be easier for me to pinch my thigh, but... you know I can't feel anything. I stroke the wall; its texture is strangely alive. I immediately draw my hand back; you never know… and then I return to the center of this room.

The brightness really appeals to me, it's so alive. There's no window, I see none, nor any bulb on the ceiling or walls. Could it be that the walls themselves are reflecting light, emitted from I know not where? Here I am inside an enigma, I'm in the heart of it, even though I'm in the middle of the room.

I play around with my wheelchair, turning it one way and another, desperately trying to understand. Then, I stop myself still, facing the field, there on the wall. The more I watch, the more I get the impression that the flowers are bending in the wind. I instinctively touch my face, it feels fresh; I frown.

There are flowers, lush grass, the sky and the sun.

There is me.

There is also this smell… created for certain by my subconscious. I breathe deeply.

I'm delving further into this haven of peace, when I notice that this light, which doesn't exist, which comes from everywhere and nowhere, casts a shadow on the ground bitterly reminding me of my condition.

A second "**ME**", made from just a dark grey outline, is keeping me company. My gaze can't break itself away from my own shadow. I have to go backwards, it depresses me this shadow! I try to hide it; but not knowing where the light comes from, I can't get rid of it. Then, as if it understood what I was aiming to do, it detaches itself from me.

It slowly begins to slide a few yards away.

Nothing is connecting us any longer; it cut the cord. How can it exist without me? I approach it now, not wanting it to leave, since this isn't something normal... My breathing quickens. I don't want to lose a piece of myself AGAIN!

Panic seems to be overwhelming me, when a click behind me brings me back to reason. Without asking, the door has opened itself wide, neither half open nor half closed... just wide open, inviting me out... politely.

My shadow has joined back onto me; we're back as ONE.

I leave this room, knowing that tomorrow I'll return. I wheel myself back to the elevator, my shadow following me closely. I don't take my eyes off it. It's different this one; too close, too dark, too normal.

Arriving on the ground floor, the door opens. This is a mandatory stop, whether we want it or not; there's nothing to see, but it stops here. Then the door automatically closes. But before it does, I place my hand on the edge of the metal door, activating the safety function, and it opens again. Facing me, the huge clock with its hands brings me back to my reality; half past six in the morning! I can't understand where the time has gone.

It's Friday today, I head to my room trying to forget what I just experienced. The answers will come by themselves tonight when I will return. My arms are working busily, I have to arrive back before Henri, if I want to avoid his questions. Catching my breath, I cast my eyes towards the floor again... my shadow still remains attached to me.

Louise watches me passing in front of the supervisors' room, I feel her gaze upon me. She alone knows what time I went out, and what time I got home. Will she hold her tongue?

I head straight to the bathroom, I can finally relax a little; Henri isn't here yet.

Like every morning, he'll open the door, ask me how I am, then inquire whether I slept well. I'll avoid that question. Then, he'll help me to have a wash and get dressed. We'll talk about everything and nothing; the weather or what it will do. For two years, Henri has taken care of me, and I don't even know whether he's married or not!

They're required not to show too much empathy.

Without knowing why, I'm feeling selfish. I'm stuck within my condition without ever asking him any questions about his life. Some things don't excuse everything...

"Hello Louie, already in the bathroom?" Henri asks, as the bedroom door closes behind him.

"Hello, I wanted to save you a bit of time."

I still wonder where the time went tonight.

He slides the bathroom door open, and stares at me.

"How was your night?"

"Banal, as usual."

He positions himself behind me and helps me to get a t-shirt. I stare in the mirror. Who is this man? Why am I asking myself this question today?

"How's your family, Henri?"

My question obviously surprises him, as he fixes me in his gaze in the mirror opposite. I don't look away.

"Why such a question?"

"Have I never asked anything about you before?"

"Why now?"

"Why not?"

"My family are fine, thank you," he said, while we do an about-turn and head for the hallway.

Suddenly, I stop my chair dead: this isn't enough, this isn't enough anymore. He goes past me, and positions himself to face me; his two muscled arms outstretching onto the armrests of my wheelchair.

"I have a little girl of four years old; we're not married, but I'm intending to ask her before our second child is born. Is your curiosity satisfied now, Louie?"

"When's the second birth due?"

"In five months' time."

"A little girl or a little boy?"

"We don't want to know."

"Okay. You'll let me know?"

"Of course. Can we go now?"

"Yes, I'm as hungry as a wolf."

Have I already spoken about Violette?
She's the flower which perfumes my thoughts. And I must
be the thistle that pricks hers.

She knows all my fears, all my joys. Violette never
complains, at least not to me, yet she could do. Violette
is my psychologist, here at the house. We have a session
once a week, the two of us, and guess what? Our session
is today! As with every Friday at eleven, just after physical
care, Violette brings me much-needed comfort after my
suffering. She has a captivating voice and soothing words,
even if it's me who says the most. She always knows the
right question to ask.

"You look a bit off-color, Louie!" she says, by way of a
greeting.

"I always appreciate your frankness. I didn't sleep..."
"Nightmares?"
"No, a promenade..."
"A promenade? Where did you go at night?"
She heads over to me. She always does it like this, she
comes from behind her desk, then just places herself in
front of me. We're as equals, we can discuss things.

"SS2."

"Again... What do you hope to find down there?"

"I don't know, I imagine a different world for myself. There isn't much left for me to dream of apart from my imagination."

"Don't say that... but wouldn't it be more prudent to activate your imagination in your bed?"

"Prudent... What am I risking down there?"

"Nothing. Maybe you'll lose yourself?"

She smiled at me.

"Lose myself... physically, or lose my mind?"

"I never said you were crazy, Louie."

She turns back around, and returns to her desk to take some notes. After a few seconds, she looks back up at me. I bring myself closer and slide my chair under her desk; face to face, with our knees touching one another's.

Equal to equal.

"Can I ask you a question, Violette?"

"You want to reverse the roles?"

"No, just one..."

She always smiles while taking notes. *'Louie becomes curious'* should be the comment of the day.

"Go ahead," she finally answers, looking up at me.

"Would you come with me one time?"

"Maybe."

I also note, at the back of my mind, that she appears curious.

"Why?"

"That's two questions!... To try to understand you a little better." She finally says.

Violette doesn't like to be questioned, no more so than Henri or anyone else working here. They shouldn't become attached to anyone; we're all temporary in this place. Us and them alike. But when the questions are asked, they answer them straightforwardly, despite all.

I'm tired from my night which I didn't notice passing by. I ask Henri kindly for permission to skip a meal; he accepts, and lies me down in my bed. My eyes close and I slip onto this highway. This dream is a recurring one... I ride, looking ceaselessly in my mirrors, I don't see the truck coming towards me. When the blackness invades my dreams, I know this is the underside of the trailer which is engulfing me. Once again I can do nothing, there's nothing I could have done.

"Louie, Louie... Wake up."

Slowly, my eyes open upon Henri's worried face, looking over me, my reality coming back to me.

"What time is it?"

"Time for dinner, and I won't let you skip a second meal."

I smile amiably.

"Do I have time for a quick shower?"

In response, he lifts me up, and we head for the bathroom. A new day begins for me, it's six o'clock in the afternoon. The water dripping onto my body gives me some degree of relief, and it wakes me up, and then I don't feel anything else. It could be freezing or burning, it would make no difference! But Henri pays attention to this kind of detail which I can no longer feel.

Henri takes very good care of me.

Twenty minutes later, I'm ready, handsome and fresh to start my night.

It's early evening; everyone says "good evening", but me I just stick to "good day". I'm out of sync with time, but nobody is paying attention. Did they even notice my absence this afternoon? We each have our own little problems. Here, we notice absences when they are longer, that's generally not a good omen at all.

Despite peas being served at dinner, the meal isn't going too badly. In any case, it doesn't break my morale, which is at a new high. I crush my vegetables into a thick and lumpy purée, which makes Henri smile.

"It makes sense," he tells me.

"I know."

I'm making my life easier, and his at the same time.

On Friday night, we watch two episodes of "*Walking dead*". Some people identify with these dead men wandering around inside a physical body which they no longer control themselves. This series just makes me smile. I knew it beforehand.

Finally, time for bed arrives; I return to my room without lying down. I have this feeling of not having left it today. I think back to Violette, and wonder when she'll join me on one of my excursions.

Everything seems calm, I push open the door of my room. Passing the supervisors' office, I nod to Louise, who's still on duty that night, and wheel myself to the elevator. It's thirteen minutes past eleven!

While the elevator takes me to SS2, I pose myself a whole load of questions. Where did the time go last night? Was it my imagination playing a trick on me or was my shadow... far from me? But, in order to have some answers, I must find the blue door again. I'm as excited as a child... or even worse!

The doors open... I hold my breath. I play with my memory and wheel myself towards my objective, head down. For once, I use the motor of my wheelchair; I have to save my strength for the rest of my night, but then I'm too impatient, I must admit. I finally find the blue door. My memory has let me down; I remain convinced that it wasn't so far away yesterday. Never mind, I found it again, and in my view that's what matters the most. Slowly, I extend my hand to the handle, it opens! Again, fully open, it invites me to enter. The same brightness emerges, it dazzles me.

I press the button and my chair enters in the room; behind me, I hear the "*clack*" of the door closing.

Tonight, the only dressed wall is covered with a mural depicting some mountains. Strangely, I'm not surprised, I move towards it, fearlessly. The fresh air is invigorating, the wall is covered with snow and is icy beneath my fingers. This room is alive! What a surreal deduction!

I turn around, I have to find the source of this light; I move around the room, slowly looking about. I can't even say that it's from the slightest nooks because there aren't any. It's perfectly square.

Soft music comes to my ears; is the room trying to calm me down?

Yesterday I was in front of the mural when my shadow broke away from me, so I position myself where I think I'm in the same place. But nothing happens. Nothing is ever as simple as we would like, unless I'd only dreamed it all, which I highly doubt. Violette did say that I wasn't crazy... so, I believe her!

I put my wheelchair in manual mode, and move a few inches, watching to see if my shadow reacts. Then, with my eyes fixed on the wall; I notice a flower protruding from the snow on the flank of the mountain; a beautiful white flower, perhaps an edelweiss. I come close to gently touching it, but just as my wheels bring me to it, it disappears. I back up straight away; I want to see it again, it's so beautiful. As soon as my arms are busy, it returns. I try once again to get closer, and it sinks back into the snow! As it doesn't want me close enough to admire this rare and beautiful flower; I take the option of staying at a suitable distance from the wall. I'd love to know its scent; another time perhaps, or maybe never. I stay to admire it for some time; here time is different so I'm not looking to estimate for how long. The clouds in the sky scatter, and the brightness becomes even more blinding. Tomorrow I'll bring my sunglasses!

As I'm looking at the wall, something else catches my eye on the floor beside me. My gaze rests right there, at the foot of my chair on my right; my shadow is moving while I'm completely immobile. I'd almost forgotten it; I was so absorbed by the flower. This time I'm not afraid, and I watch what it does.

Slowly, it detaches from me, like yesterday.

Slowly, I watch it become autonomous.

It glides gently and is identical to that which I am; a man in a wheelchair. Now, it's several yards away from me. I firmly hold the arms of my chair, my fingers clenching over; yet my shadow stretches like I did upon waking, beforehand. It raises itself, it does whatever it has the urge to do or feel. It comes to life!

I'm no longer alone in this room. My eyes widen at the spectacle, which my other self is presenting to me.

Now, *Led Zeppelin's "Whole Lotta Love"* arrives at my ears; I'm not dreaming, this place is looking to win me over, this is my favorite song! Otherwise there's another option; I'm going completely crazy.

My shadow stands up and succeeds at that which I'm no longer capable of doing. With the strength of its arms, it climbs out of the chair, stretching its legs, aching from so much inactivity for so long. How is this possible? I'm here watching, enviously.

The empty wheelchair slowly fades from my sight.

My shadow takes a step towards the wall; this time the flower doesn't disappear. It keeps walking, slightly swaying to the rhythm of music.

I move my wheelchair a little; my shadow, so far away, doesn't follow me. It is autonomous, it doesn't even turn back towards me, reaching its arms out to the edelweiss. I see its hand delicately seize the flower; my shadow is holding the shadow of the flower in its hand! Incredible. It brings it up to its nose... I instinctively make the same gesture; it's my turn to follow my shadow. The world is reversed... The scent fills my nostrils and intoxicates me.

The shadow is only a shadow; I can't see its face, just its contours, like any self-respecting shadow: after all, that's normal.

It shrinks before my eyes; it gently places one foot inside the scene on the wall, and then the other, placing its hands against the edges of the wall, which opens up to it. Its entire body is now part of the landscape. It turns back and forth, contemplating the scene within.

I feel a cool breeze on my face.

I see my shadow start to climb the mountain, as if nothing mattered, with our flower in its hand

I feel the cold; it invades me, goes right through me, and my body shivers. My legs are hurting for the first time in ages: I can feel them! I put my hands on them to soothe the pain that shouldn't be; which cannot be.

How would you feel if, in your pajamas, you started to climb a snowy mountain? Your feet frozen, the tips of your fingers numb, seeing the breath coming from your mouth, all this without forgetting the fact that you haven't used your legs for so long that the muscles are now lacking! But at this moment, I don't give a damn about all those details.

I'm living in this moment of grace; I walk with my head held high, in the middle of the wall, thanks to my shadow. And believe me; it's enjoyable to be able to do this, BUT especially to feel it, because it's good that it's happening. I can feel in my legs, all of my shadow's effort during its ascent. It seems to do this without any difficulty, whereas I'm bursting with agony; but it's good!

I'm running out of breath, of strength, of energy, but it's not giving up. Sometimes it turns its head towards me as if to check what's happening to its half-dead body. What it's seeing must satisfy it, because it carries on. And if I demanded it to stop, would it obey me?

The air in my lungs is missing, not because of my poor physical condition, but because of the altitude. The music is making my head spin; the fresh air too. The room is spinning around me, I feel myself parting from its whirlwind before I've finished climbing.

I can hear a distant voice telling me:

"That's enough for today..."
Then the darkness takes me over.

My eyes open painfully upon a room which I don't know.

I slowly drag myself out of this black hole which envelopes me, feeling upset because I don't know when was the last time that I was conscious. Bit by bit, the events come back to me.

As though my eyelids were connected to an alarm, a few seconds after my eyes first blink, I can distinguish a nurse entering the room. She comes towards me, looks at the apparatus around me, and finishes off by moving a little light over my eyes, going from one to the other, without a moment's doubt to herself that she's making me suffer horribly. Next, she introduces something into my ear; she's torturing me! Finally, she leans towards me and gently readjusts my sheets.

"Your fever died down, that's very good. The doctor will come to see you, prepare for a sermon," she says, in conclusion, tucking me in; and then she leaves the room giving me no time to retort.

I feel that I'm helpless in this bed. I'm missing something.

Through the window, the landscape which is presented before my eyes, which I've looked at since I first arrived in this place a few years earlier, is at least something familiar.

My head is in a vice, an indescribable pain reminds me that there are still parts of my body which I can feel. I'm trying to stop thinking about last night, that one to which I don't know the ending. But what I am sure of, is what I did see. Not to mention what I felt in my spine and the muscles in my legs, while climbing the mountain; of that I am certain. It was too good! But at this exact moment, my head feels like exploding. I clamp my hands onto my skull and I can feel the thing that's compressing me. My head really is in a vice, they've immobilized it! Why?

Someone pushes the door open in a way which is uncommon; or perhaps too common for me: using a foot-rest to open it.

She comes over to me, frowning; she's unhappy, by all appearances.

"It seems that I'd asked you to be careful, Louie."

Violette is there, right in front of me. Almost equal-to-equal.

"Would you please explain this?"

"We found you lying on the ground in the second basement, don't you remember?"

"Did you see the room?"

"You were in the laundry room in the north wing."

"No," I reply, frowning in my turn.

That room wasn't a laundry, and moreover I was in the west wing; I keep repeating it to myself. Not to convince myself, but in order not to forget.

"Yes, it's exactly there that we found you. In falling, you hit your head and now have concussion. You didn't need this, believe me!"

That explains why my head is imprisoned.

I attempt a third question.

"What day is it today?"

"It happened four days ago."

"Four days! You found me four days ago?"

"That's basically what I just said. How do you feel?"

"I have a hell of a headache. I don't understand, Violette," I say, trying to move something other than my eyes.

"What don't you understand?"

"The time."

"You fell into a sort of coma after your fall. You woke up just this morning."

"Did you see the room yourself?"

"Uh, no; why would I go to SS2 to see the laundry?"

"I wasn't in the laundry. Believe me Violette, please!"

"Nevertheless, it was there that we found you. Why does this point trouble you?"

I just whisper:

"It was not the laundry."

She gives me a worried look.

"How do you call that room then?" she asks, in a very soft voice.

I look outside, I'm not crazy. But, how could I explain the inexplicable?

"I don't know. You're not able to understand. You have to see it to believe it," I say, staring at her once again.

"Believe what?"

"That I wasn't in the laundry."

She drags her chair to the window and starts talking to me again.

"In falling to the ground, you severely banged your head. Maybe you don't remember where you were."

I can't yell at her that I was in the midst of climbing a mountain. That my shadow was holding an edelweiss; I'd love to offer her that. That I felt so alive even though it was so hard. That my body was reacting to the cold, that the music intoxicated me. I can't tell her all that. Not now. I must show her, unless I want to end up in the wing for people who've lost their minds following an accident.

"Perhaps you're right after all," I say, simply, keeping to myself everything I could have told her.

She turns her wheelchair towards me, smiling, and comes back over to my bed. The sun is blinding me as much as her smile.

"That's much wiser Louie. I'll let you rest. In a few days you'll go back to your own room. I'll come and see you there. In the meantime, try to get some sleep."

She finishes her sentence with a touch on my arm; a gentle stroke. Then she leaves. Before she reaches the door, I persist and ask her the question again.

"Will you accompany me there someday?"

She turns back around.

"Maybe. Sleep now."

Always the same reply.

They finally bring me back to my room; for ten days I was stuck in intensive care due to a fall that never existed, at least in my memory.

Last Sunday, my parents visited me like almost every weekend. My mother cried when she saw me. I tried to explain to her that I was feeling well, in vain; and that if I was still here, it was just because they didn't want me to be going back promenading around in SS2, or 1 for that matter, alone at night. I couldn't tell them anything about what I experienced down there. That remains my secret.

I'll have to take Violette with me, and then she would see and believe me! But for the moment, mum's the word.

A lot of time has passed since my last trip, but my memory is intact on what I saw and felt in that room with the blue door.

A memorandum has been created especially for me. I swear; I saw it on returning to my room. They didn't go so far as to put my picture on it, as if I was a fugitive on the run. But my name is written largely enough that the supervisors don't forget about me; but above all don't let me go for a wander at night. I'm under close supervision, which doesn't suit my plans!

This morning, it's not Henri who crosses the threshold of my door with a smile, but a big hefty man who I don't know. He's not very cheerful, this one, and he doesn't give me the urge to get to know him. I refrain from asking him questions. We exchange the minimum necessary courtesies to remain polite.

This said, I hope that Henri isn't in trouble because of me.

At noon, I eat almost nothing. It was difficult and this guy, who seems more like a torturer than a caregiver, doesn't seem very willing to help me. Nevertheless; if he remains with me, he'll have to change his spots, because he's not a very big help to me, in addition to not being amiable.

It's the beginning of the afternoon; I take myself around the corridors of this institution. The rain hits the picture-windows. Autumn has set in for real now. Soon, leaves will cover the ground, bringing me additional difficulties. This is the kind of detail that we never think about when we walk, with our feet, on a carpet of leaves. We find it rather pretty, or even fun to kick our feet about in them. For me, it's one more obstacle.

I feel a certain paranoia come over me, and keep looking back to see if I'm being followed. But I don't notice anything. The guidelines they received, relate particularly to the night-time. That doesn't please me at all!

My wheels take me to the elevator. I look all around me and press the call button. Do you ever feel irresistibly drawn to something? This is what's happening to me now. SS2 lights up beneath my fingers. My heart is pounding with curiosity and excitement. If I could tap my feet with impatience, I would do.

Like a child, I launch myself from the elevator in all haste, eager to get to the blue door. My arms are busy turning my wheels, I'm scouring the corridors in a search for my reward. For more than ten days, I've dreamt of this moment. I'm curious to see what the room has in store for me today. What will the beautiful landscape be, that it will present to me? Without thinking, I look at the ground; my shadow is there, faithfully at its post. That room is Machiavellian; it moves constantly. I can't explain this, nor so many other things, but I find that I'm empty-handed after the first part of my exploration. I haven't lost hope so I start on the northern corridor. I've never seen any other blue door, just that one. I can't miss it. Disappointed, I complete this corridor; I haven't yet seen it. I have tears in my eyes. I have a final look around, but it doesn't appear! It's trying to drive me mad.

I go back to the elevator and stop at SS1; who knows, maybe during the daytime, the room is there? After another hour of searching, I have to face the facts; it's not findable. I'll have to find a ploy in order to get out of my room this same night without being noticed. An idea comes to mind, just as the door opens, facing the big clock on the ground floor; it's ten minutes past six in the afternoon. I still have some time before dinner; I head to the office for consultations.

I knock softly on the door; no response. I'm decidedly angry that nothing is going as I'd like this afternoon. Alongside the picture-windows, I can see her outside, right there. The rain has stopped and she's parked near a bench a few feet away, behind the glass. She's reading.

I hasten over to join her.

"I need you..."

I almost shout.

"Hello, Louie. What's the matter?" She says, looking up from her book.

"Hello, sorry..." I say, looking down.

I feel ashamed for such rudeness.

"So?" She insists.

"I need to go out tonight."

"To go back and fracture your skull again?"

"Noooo."

I bring myself a bit closer up to her.

"Come with me, Violette, please."

She looks at me with a frown. I'll have to watch my words or I'll end up in the asylum, but if she comes, she'll believe me. She puts her book in her lap. She knows I won't give up.

"What's at the bottom of this Louie?"

"If I tell you, you won't believe me, so I want to show you."

"You just need me to be able get out. You're being watched and you know it."

"It's not just that, I'd already asked you to accompany me before this restriction!"

"That's a bit much, Louie. We're not restricting you, we're protecting you."

"Prove it to me then!"

"We'll see, I had something planned tonight. You know I have a life outside of this Centre."

"I know very well. Just once, Violette; come with me, please."

I feel that maybe she's giving in.

"I'll think about it. Now I have to go, sorry."

I look away. After a few yards, she turns to face me one last time.

"Be careful, we all love you," she says, simply.

"See you tonight, Violette."

"Maybe..."

The sliding door closes itself behind her. It starts to rain and I'm wet, but I have hope.

I'm here in front of my plate, to play with the fries; it's Thursday today. Nothing amuses me. The big guy is here too, he's always hanging on my coat-tails, and by all evidence he doesn't like mayonnaise like Henri does. He just gives me the honor of his presence, he isn't helping me at all. Did he receive an order to give me a hard life? Have they not noticed how hard it already was for me, since that fateful Sunday when my life changed dramatically with this wheelchair?

He presumes that my meal is over and pushes me, without asking my opinion, to the TV room. Great; we'll be stuck with a super reality-TV program. They would do better to come and film here, where our realities are much less entertaining than those which they're showing us. I heard one day, that all those people were merely actors. That they were paid to kill each other verbally, to love, to eat, and all that in front of us. Do we look so miserable in our own lives? How many people pay to vote for so-and-so to stay in a program, which in any case has already been pre-written? I still have hope that we might have a good film.

Despite everything around me, my mind is still stuck on just one thing. The blue door! I regularly turn my head towards the hallway, hoping to see Violette's wheelchair rolling over to me.

One hour after the start of the show, I'm so bored that I turn my wheelchair around to escape. I only manage a quarter turn, when I feel hands gripping the handles.

"I'll take you back to your room," says the big guy.

There's no emotion in his voice, just a little light relief, knowing that his work is almost done for today. He'll be able to go freely to join the outside world.

"Thanks."

He puts me in my bed without any sensitivity, and lays the sheets back over me. A mechanical action without much affection, believe me. His gaze is empty; this guy is as cold as a sociopath.

"Could you give me the TV remote control, please?"

Without a word, he hands it to me. I thank him sufficiently with a nod. I turn over to a different channel to the other room, and watch him go, frowning.

"Where are you going with my chair?" I ask, worriedly.

"I'm taking it into the supervisors' room. There are orders."

"Whose orders?"

"From your doctor."

"Which one?"

He turns back towards me.

"Who cares, I follow them; that's all"

I take back what I said; he isn't a sociopath, but a psychopath!

"You know, if I was able to get out of my bed on my own... just to walk to this chair, which is usually left in the corner of my room. Well! You know what?"

He looks at me in surprise, awaiting what's to follow.

"I'd be at home, not here trying to have a normal life! Go away with my chair and never come back. See MY doctor, the same one who gave an order this absurd, and tell him that I don't want to see you again. NOT EVER."

He doesn't respond to these words; he walks away, carrying with him my hopes of escape.

It's a long time since I've shouted at someone. I look at my room; I've never found it so shabby since I arrived. I've never been so desperate since I arrived here. I'm trapped in a body that's partly inactive, and now I really am aware of it for the first time.

I'm powerless.

I now better understand my mother's tears, the look of pity from my ex-girlfriend, or my father's multiple taps on my shoulders, saying *"So how's my big guy?"* I understand all that now. For an hour, I ponder my rage, clenching my fingers on the sheets, grinding those of my muscles which work. An hour with my eyes on the TV without really watching it. An hour in which I realize that, from now on, my life will be like this; at the mercy of others...

Violette slowly enters the room; I don't hear her coming. Wheels make less noise than footsteps do, on the floor.

"Where's your chair, Louie?"

I raise my eyes, misted up with tears, towards her.

"Confiscated."

"For heaven's sake, who did that?"

"If there was any form of love or mercy from heaven, it would make itself known, Violette. Excuse me for telling you."

She comes over to the bed... and me, gently. She puts her hand on my arm, it's the first time Violette has shown affection towards me.

"Sequestering is now the in-word?"

"I'm sorry, Louie."

"Do you agree with that?"

"No, of course not."

I lean over towards her.

"Help me please."

She looks right at me. I watch her pupils shift from one eye to the other. She leans over and grabs the bell: as she plunges her gaze into mine, she presses the button. I hear footsteps approaching my room, heavy ones.

He arrives.

She does two perfect rotations to extricate herself and deal with the person who is coming.

"Who gave the order to remove the wheelchair from the room?" She asks, in a tone which surprises me.

A man, whose name I didn't know, stands there in front of her. This isn't my torturer.

"Dr Parker, ma'am."

Finally some answers!

"Bring the wheelchair back here, immediately!"

"But..."

"Please," she adds.

"Okay Doctor, right away."

Without another word, he leaves. Violette doesn't turn back towards me; we wait and listen. I don't know what to think. The man comes back pushing MY chair, that part of me that you can't just steal from me with such ease; I won't accept this anymore. He's about to put it in its place, but Violette says:

"Put him into it, please."

The man doesn't reply, and carries out her orders. I let him lift me without a word, then he goes away flabbergasted, visibly displeased.

"Let's go before I change my mind," she adds, positioning her wheelchair control to '*on*'.

Violette's hair lifts up as her chair glides towards the hallway, and the elevators. Passing in front of the supervisors' room, I don't give them even one glance. I avoid facing the gaze of those who were keeping me prisoner. Arriving in the hall, she finally stops, turns to me and bursts out laughing.

"No; but did you see the face he was pulling?"

I don't reply. This isn't a game!

"Louie, relax!"

"Easy for you to say. That said; thank you."

She comes over to me and, for the second time today, rests her hand on my arm. Her warmth runs through me like an electric current, going to nestle where I wasn't expecting it.

"What would you like show me in SS2?"

I'm staring at her, wondering if she too had felt something inside.

"Come on," I say, simply.

Now, here we are in the elevator. I let her press the button. Our descent is carried out smoothly and in silence. Gallant that I am; I let her out first.

"I'll follow you," she says.

"We need to find a blue door."

"How is it that we need to find it? Don't you know where we're going?"

While I'm making my way into the corridor, I turn around and give her a glance.

"The room moves around!"

She frowns. She doesn't believe me! But she ends up following me... finally, and will eventually believe me. After each new corridor, after every turn, I pray that the door will appear. I hope it won't play a trick on me this afternoon, or Violette will take me for a complete moron. For half an hour, we go around and around in vain. She sighs, she's becoming impatient... At last, the blue door appears. I specifically say "appears" because this is the second time that we've passed by here. I stop myself in front of it, nervously. Violette switches her gaze from the door back to me. She says nothing. She knows very well that it wasn't here on our previous pass along this corridor. I operate the handle; it opens instantly, not half-way but fully, just as always.

It invites us to enter.

I emerge into this blinding light to which I am now accustomed. Not hearing the "*clack*" of it closing, I turn around. Violette isn't following me.

"Come on in."

"What is this place?"

"Come in," I say again, offering her my hand.

She's barely crossed the threshold of the door when it closes, emitting a small discreet "*clack*". Soft music flows over us. A piano melody, barely perceptible, but present nonetheless, and soothing.

The room is different. Would it be intimidated by Violette's visit? The wall where, every time, it gives pride of place to a landscape, is completely blank.

She brings me out of my daydream.

"Where does this light come from? I can't see any bulb or source for it," she asks me.

"I still haven't solved that mystery."

"And the music? It's not the same one as the hospital's."

"What kind of music do you like Violette?"

"This kind, exactly this kind. It appeases me."

The room is in the act of charming Violette!

"Was it here, where you fell?"

"I have no memory of falling, only of having been enveloped, or of going into a black hole, to describe it more accurately, yes."

"Really? Explain it to me Louie, please."

"There isn't much to explain. I have no answer to this phenomenon. The thing I can tell you is that last time, the music which was playing here was one of my favorite songs."

"And now you believe it's playing for me," she said, thoughtfully, looking everywhere around her.

"I'm sure of it."

This blank wall is worrying me; I gently approach it. It's different, I think the light is coming from this wall. My hand brushes gently against it; again I have this feeling that it's alive. Violette comes over to me, I hear her wheeling along as if the ground was something else than a tiled floor.

"The first time I came here, on this wall was a field of flowers; they were so fragrant. The second time, a snowy mountain greeted me, I even picked an edelweiss... I was cold, so cold," I conclude, watching Violette.

She's staring at me, with her profound look. Then, I notice the silence; the music has stopped.

My gaze rests upon the wall, at the bottom, a line is rising. I'm looking for as best a view as I can get. The line isn't straight, nor is it curved... Next, forms slowly appear, and then colors. I slowly move myself away from it, no longer touching it; the line now stops!

"Violette, look..."

I play with my hand, taking the risk that the line will no longer play with me, so as to show her that these things couldn't be explained by words. The incredible isn't always explainable... She moves herself away from the wall; from fear perhaps. My hand is still in contact with it, but the line stops itself; the colors now fade. I turn towards Violette.

"Come back here," I say, panting.

The wall wants us; both of us!

She returns hesitantly; she seems to be having trouble with her wheelchair. I look at the ground: the white color has now become white sand... What a nightmare it is to wheel along in the sand, but she's strong and is able to get back to me. The line continues to rise, I start to see the more tangible shapes of a beach forming before our eyes. But the wall has been extending itself; the ground is part of the scene, and this is so for the first time.

The room takes possession of us.

The regular sound of the waves replaces the music. In the sky, a seagull passes. Its cry, pushed seaward by the wind, fades away. The scene becomes complete: dunes, sea, and an azure sky. There's good weather on this deserted beach.

I turn to Violette, her face immobilized by the surprising landscape which just came to be drawn before her, before us. She remains silent, a small temporary handicap, after that which she's just witnessed.

How would she believe me without seeing it? I wonder what surprises her the most; the unrealism of this moment, or the beauty of the landscape?

Now that the scene is set, I move back a little, as best as I can, being careful not to get bogged-down in the sand. I leave Violette to her contemplation for a little bit longer. While my eyes go to the young woman on the horizon, the fresh wind makes my cheeks blush; I can feel it. I'm standing a few yards from the wall, which can be discovered by those who would wish to follow me.

What's going on in her psychologist's head? How will she explain it rationally?

I look at my shadow, which remains well-behaved for the moment.

My therapist turns towards me, she smiles at me.

"Come here," I say, softly.

With difficulty, she removes her gaze from the wall and joins me again. We're now facing the wall. The sea air makes us feel good. It fills our lungs and ventilates our minds.

My eyes come to rest on the sand, undulating at my feet; at last my shadow moves itself. I put my hand on Violette's, she stares at me, frowning. My eyes guide hers towards the ground, her reaction is immediate; her hand grasps onto mine.

"What is it?"

"Shhh..." I whisper.

My shadow stretches out before us, it stretches as if we're waking up. Slowly, it goes over to the beach and turns back around. It offers its hand to Violette's. Her shadow still hesitates, slightly timidly! I look at my other self. I'm not really used to watching it go its own way; then I watch Violette's eyes widen more and more as and when her shadow detaches from her.

What we're living here, now, gets us together. It creates an intimacy between us, and this is only the beginning. Our hands are still linked, my fingers reddening under her pressure, but I won't let go of this last link to reality. I hope her heart can hold up.

The second shadow doesn't dare to venture far from its owner. It's torn between joining my shadow's invitation, and being itself. It's stuck at the bottom of the dunes, hesitating... still.

"Let it go... release it"

"I'm afraid..."

"What it can happen?"

"This is so..."

"... Far from what you can explain, I know."

Then she lets it go. It begins taking some steps, with its head down watching its feet. Then suddenly, it blossoms, with arms outstretched. And everything starts... I'm stunned to see 'her' running towards me. Violette bursts out laughing... A nervous laugh, a laugh of joy. You should know that she was born with her disability, she would never have dreamed of doing even a single step one day. I see her rubbing her legs, there in her wheelchair: those limbs which she can now feel, for the first time in her life, with a smile on her lips.

'She' runs so fast that she stumbles and finds herself in the arms of my shadow, which barely catches her. Slowly, mine stands her up. They find themselves entwined. The situation becomes comical, I'd never imagined holding her in my arms, and not for the lack of having dreamed of it. 'She' pulls herself together and dusts off her clothes. How happy I am to see this, to give her these moments, even if I've done nothing other than find this place... maybe magical.

My shadow takes her hand; shadows are only shadows, but here in our chairs, our two faces light up following this little bit of this other universe. Their way of walking, moving... body language here takes on its full dimensions. Here they go; climbing up a dune, I can feel it in my calves! They breathe deeply, it can be seen by their chests heaving. At the top, they face the ocean... the waves coming to their deaths in a perpetual motion on the sand.

The sun caresses our faces, this warmth is very real.

The wind gently lifts Violette's long hair, bringing to my nostrils this scent which I know so well, from noticing it each time I go into her office. But here, this fragrance intoxicates me; a blend of lavender and vanilla. I close my eyes.

Like a guillotine, Violette's phone rings in the room. Instantly, everything disappears! The grains of sand fly away, the gulls depart, to fly to and fro across another sky... Everything has gone; suddenly I feel sad to have lost what I was going through. She looks at me... looking sorry too.

A *clack* sounds behind us; the room is driving us out... Would it be angry with this interruption?

Two days had passed since our escapade on the beach. Two days that Violette hadn't said a word to me. The room chucked us out like undesirables; this had shocked, but also disappointed, my therapist. So, she cloistered herself in her office in "*total*" silence. On her door, a sign saying "*do not disturb*" took me aback. She's also cancelled all her appointments.

They lifted the surveillance they'd placed on me a few days earlier. I took the opportunity to go for a small trip out last night, but I didn't find the room with the blue door. It's avoiding me, I'm sure!

It's half past two. After a good meal in the company of Henri, I've moved myself into the library. I'm pleased with Henri's return, and that everything has gone back to normal. After all, I was quite worried and I didn't deserve to be harassed here!

I try to focus on the detective novel which the librarian recommended to me, but I must confess that I cannot: it isn't very good. But I have a principle of always finishing a book which I've started, as a matter of respect towards the author. But I'm dragging it out now, rereading sentences several times; my task is complicated.

A hand is placed upon my shoulder, freeing me from the scant attention that I'd had on the words. Turning my head slightly, I recognize the slender fingers of Violette. Without a hello, she invites me to follow her, which I do in silence. On the way out from this place, which is devoted to words and to silence, I ask her:

"Where are we going?"

"Into the psychiatry wing," she announces.

This information freezes my blood.

"Uh! Violette?"

She turns and smiles at me.

"Not for us, don't be silly!"

"That reassures me, so then why?"

"We're going to meet someone."

"Who?"

"You'll see; stop with your questions and follow me."

She is very kind, Violette; if only I could read into her thoughts! She shows no signs of life for forty-eight hours, even forbids others from approaching; and now here she's almost kidnapping me and taking me to the madhouse. I hate that word; to me those people just have a different view of things. Some are really crazy of course, but here at the institute that's not the same thing.

Here we are wheeling down the corridors alongside the picture-window. Outside, the wind is ravaging the trees; the leaves no longer have any hope of staying attached to their branches. The separation is sudden but inevitable.

I'm trying to keep up with Violette, who could win the Paralympic games today! What energy this girl has, and what strength!

In the heavily guarded entrance to the P-wing, Violette shows her credentials and asks to see someone called Christian, I don't remember his surname. I wait behind her. A big strapping guy comes over to us and asks us to follow him. We meet no-one in the corridors except for some caregivers.

Here, it's very quiet, here it's different.

I wouldn't want to stay here!

We stop outside a door, the man opens a small door viewer like those in prison doors, and announces us. At least the resident still has the choice. He allows us to come in, which we do in silence. The big guy closes the door with a double lock; I feel a bit "*claustrophobic*" trapped in this room. Him, he waits outside, well I do hope so. We never know what could happen. We are in P-wing!

This room surprises me. It's something other than I'd imagined it, when I was outside its door. The interior resembles my own room. The difference is, more than just the door: there are bars across the window.

Outside, the wind continues wreaking its destruction.

This man is in a wheelchair too, he doesn't seem crazy... not at all. We greet each other amiably. I let Violette talk to him; I don't even know why we're here.

"We have to talk about the room with the blue door. What can you tell us about it?"

The man, Christian, stares hard at us.

"Do you believe me now?" He replied, calmly.

"I believe you, yes, and I apologize for not having done so before."

The man's expression changes; he leans towards Violette, opening his eyes widely. I'm going to maybe revise my view of madness having seen his look.

"You found it too?"

"It's Louie who discovered this room, in SS2."

He looks at me, I smile at him. What else could I do?

"Tell us about it Christian, please."

He sits down properly, sighing, fiddling with his fingers... manhandling them.

"In the beginning, it was beautiful. I was watching myself flying with the birds again. That which I could no longer do, since my hang-gliding accident," he says, looking at and massaging his legs.

"And?" Violette asks, impatient to know what was coming next.

"The birds spoke to me. I was travelling. This room gave me what I hoped the most for on this earth. Then, little by little..."

Beads of sweat were beginning to well up on his forehead.

He fell silent and drank some water before continuing.

"During some months, I explored many places; some more beautiful than others. It became a real obsession for me to get myself there. I no longer ate any more, I was just waiting for one thing: for the sun to set!"

"Little by little what, Christian?"

He looks up to her, his eyes misted with tears. This memory, which has been revived, overwhelms him; finally he speaks:

"The wall engulfed me within my worst nightmares..."

The man didn't seem crazy, but shocked. Anyone who would listen to his story, would intern him. Maybe it was better this way, for his own safety.

"What kind of nightmares?" Asks Violette.

"Those which nobody would want to live through. But in that room you don't have the choice, the door only opens again when it decides to! Then, there are the voices... asking, pleading..."

"What voices?"

Violette gives me a quizzical gaze, I divert mine, and avoid telling her that I'd heard a voice.

"Of those who are stuck!" he continued.

Violette looks at him, puzzled, trying to distinguish the true parts from the false; the madness from the reality. She places her hand on the man's arm.

"We'll let you rest, Christian. Thank you very much."

"I know you take me for a madman. Beware, or else they will lock you up in here with me. At a certain point, there's no turning back. You'll have to make a choice. I chose not to follow the voice."

Violette is already knocking at the door to leave, the big strapping guy opens it, and we leave while Christian continues to warn us.

I hear shouting as the heavy door closes.

"Make the right choice! Don't do as I did..."

We move ourselves slowly away from Christian; a final sentence comes to my ears.

"Follow the voice, what have you to lose!" I finally perceive. Then tears, quite distinct and real.

Violette looks at me, I'm not the only one to have heard him.

The big strapping guy comes back to the door of the P-wing. Before going out, I turn around one last time, and I see him running towards the room of a man who hasn't lost his head, no; but who got stuck on his hopes, and regrets his choice so much.

We wheel silently along past the picture-windows; same route, same view of chaos coming from outside. It's good to be inside in the warm.

I don't know what to think about our interview and I question myself a lot. How did Violette know about this man? I stop dead, I need to know.

"You'd heard about the room before me, is that right?"

She stops, and stands facing me.

"Yes, long ago. I wasn't sure, it took me some time to retrieve his file."

"I thought you were angry with me, Violette."

"No, I wanted to know, that's all. Have you also heard the voices, Louie?"

I avert my eyes, I don't know what to say to her.

"Louie?"

"Once, yes."

I refrain from telling her that the words still resound in my head.

"Were they menacing?"

"Not at all, then I thought it was my imagination. It only happened once."

"What did they say?"

"There was only one. It just said that it was enough for that day, and the door reopened."

"That's it?"

"Yes, just that. Nothing more fantastic!"

She remained silent, staring at the swirling leaves behind the glass.

"We'll return..." she said, finally.

"Is that a question or a statement?"

"Both."

I approach very closely to her, as close as our wheelchairs permit us to. With my hand, I turn her face towards me; her skin is soft. Her calmness shows in her eyes.

"You're not afraid?"

"No, and I'm still a scientist. I have to explain things to myself. "

This excuse isn't bad, nevertheless it's still an excuse to me.

"You're not curious? Do you sincerely believe that there's something scientific in all this?"

She looks at me... but doesn't respond; I've touched a nerve. I watch her gently place her hand on the wheelchair's operating joystick. She still doesn't say a word, but moves off. I follow her. Arriving at the elevator, she finally says:

"To get some answers, we must go back there!"

"At this hour, the door won't show itself."

"Why?"

"Not in the afternoon, that's all. It's a fact which I've established."

"Let's try anyway. There's no logic to it all, so..."

She smiles without finishing her sentence. Then, she presses the call button on the elevator. She's made her decision, and nothing, not even me, would be able to change her mind.

What we saw and heard from Christian didn't scare her; on the contrary, it aroused her curiosity a bit more. The room with the blue door is hypnotic; Violette must now understand my fascination for it, not to mention my obsession. But to see her like this scares me; her eyes remain the same, but not her self-restraint. She's losing control. I prefer to follow her. Not to leave her alone in this quest. Not to leave her alone in that room. The voices could take her away forever.

I'll have to tell her, one day...

The room gives us hope. It makes us live and feel things we cannot live... for the moment. If we believe Christian, things could degenerate, and then, what will be our worst nightmare in common, Violette and I?

We've already reached the point of no return, it haunts us, obsesses us. It's completely besieging our minds. We're aware of it, but we let it continue; therein lies the true danger. That room builds on our misfortune, our handicap. I realized this after my first visit. I'm deeply buried in my thoughts when Violette brings me back to reality.

"Are you coming or not?"

She appears slowly in front of me, she holds the elevator doors. I look at her, I mustn't stop looking at her; her gaze, her posture. If I can't save myself, at least I have to try to protect her!

"Of course I'm coming! You don't get rid of me that easily."

I'm near to her, trying to think of something apart from the negative aspects of the room. Christian's words are well anchored in my head. I must be on my guard, someone must do that for the both of us.

She pushes the button and we descend towards the SS2. A few seconds later, the doors open and we find ourselves directly in front of the blue door. For the first time, it's actually waiting for us. Did it know that we were coming?

"You see..." she says, with an odd smile of satisfaction.

She's already heading for the door, which opens, emitting a small, well familiar, "*Clack*" noise. The door opens fully before us, it's inviting us once again into its lair. I try to look inside it, but the brightness is even stronger than usual; a great white light awaits us. Without hesitation, Violette commits to entering, I can't even hold her back. I, in my turn, enter; the second, equally familiar "*clack*" closes the door on reality.

Violette glides over towards the wall, she's only come once before and yet her actions are already well established. I follow her, like a little dog... Will I be able to protect her? Doubts overcome me. We're dazzled. A powerful aura surrounds us, blinding us. Little by little, this fades and the wall finally appears...

The blinding light fades and, slowly, the darkness envelops us. For the first time in the room, it's night. A dark night, almost frightening.

I hear Violette getting close to me.

Christian's words still echo in the background in my head; a little alarm bell, which in addition to the blackness really doesn't reassure me. Then I turn my attention back to the wall. If the room has shown itself so quickly, to be so available, it's because something is going to happen.

My gaze is lost in the darkness; meanwhile, stars are appearing. First, a little speck in this universe, then a glow is born, then finally here we are, encircled by a starry sky. This allows me to see Violette's dazzling face. It's true that it's beautiful, this reflection of the stars in the blue of her eyes; such sparks of life! A crescent moon is gradually emerging from behind a cloud, driven by the wind. Space, infinity; the grandeur of all and nothing. The stars are everywhere, even under our wheels, it's making me a bit dizzy, being suspended in this way in the void. Evidently so for Violette too, because she takes my hand;

more precisely, she grabs it, but it's not painful. One of the stars is becoming larger, it gets closer, whiter, brighter, and flattens itself out. From now on it resembles a plateau.

Looking more closely, I notice hands gripping onto the rim of this flat saucer. Then gently by the strength of its arms, a shadow rises above it. Our own shadows haven't moved, we have visitors here in this improbable place! It stands up, it's a man! He positions himself facing us. I see his hand distinctly offered towards us, and with his index finger, he beckons us to join him. For the first time, I feel my shadow detach itself from me, I feel it and I suffer. This separation is tearing all around me, as if someone was amusing themselves by removing my skin. Suddenly, my whole body rises and then falls back onto my chair, it has left. Forgetting my pain, I watch it freely making headway towards the platform. What would've happened if I'd fought to keep back this inseparable part of me?

"Have you felt any pain, Violette?"

"Why would I feel pain?"

"Forget it…"

"Are you okay, Louie?" She asks me, putting pressure on my hand and looking at the wall.

My raw flesh is burning me, her pressure is tyrannizing me. Such pain! I look at my hand in the light of the moon, my skin is still there; all this was only an impression, yet a very realistic illusion of the scale of my pain. I'm not dwelling on this, otherwise maybe I'll become truly mad. Christian didn't mention physical pain in his experience. Maybe we should've questioned him a little further.

I try to forget this, which isn't really happening, and come back to the wall. At present there are three of us on the star; the other shadow is fading, I find myself alone with Violette.

A piano melody and then a female voice come to my ears. A beautiful and dramatic piece that I know so well. It was our song, my girlfriend and I, before. How does the room know that? Millions of memories of my previous life come back to flash before me, but my shadow doesn't care. It's living in the present moment and invites Violette's shadow to dance.

The two shadows embrace and begin to move themselves in this magical setting. Standing firmly on both legs, they're carried along by the music. Meanwhile my heart is pounding, never would I have imagined the present moment! Is this what Violette wanted too?

I come to realize how much I would love to hold Violette in my arms like this. To be able to whisper words in her ear, to hug her and hold her against me.

In the end, this room is cruel!

Then, as they slowly spin around to the rhythm of the song, which repeats itself endlessly, one question comes to me, killing all the magic of the moment: What does it want in return? Suddenly, while I'm wondering to myself, a flash of light pierces the sky, violent and dangerous, startling our shadows. Violette's one snuggles against me even more, I feel her fear. I protect her with my arms and cradle her head in the crook of my shoulder. A second flash touches her shadow, it detaches itself from me.

Could the room be jealous?

I look carefully at her shadow, it seems to be alright. Can a shadow die? A third flash pierces it; my shadow rushes towards hers. This time her shadow collapses, I kneel beside it and turn its head towards my physical self.

Here, her hand has let go of mine.

"Violette?"

I turn myself towards her, her head is resting gently on her shoulder... unconscious or perhaps worse.

"Stop this for pity's sake!"

I hear myself shouting. This is unrealistic. My words echo around the room, everything disappears. Here we are once again in the blinding light; I need some moments to be able to distinguish Violette near to me. Our shadows are in their places, without pain. She isn't doing well at all. Her pulse is weak. A "*clack*" resounds behind me, the room releases us. How can I get Violette out of here? It's not as though I could carry her! Then an idea comes to me; I turn her chair around, thanking God that it's electric. I position it facing the door and the elevators, which I can see. Our exit door gives us a hand. Well in position now, I press the button and her wheelchair slowly makes its way. I let her cross the threshold and start heading there myself too. Her chair bangs against the metal doors of the elevator, but at least she's outside, safely. I lower my head, not wishing to see Violette's head swaying whenever her chair touches the metal.

"*CLACK*"...

I raise my head again; the door has closed itself.

I'm still trapped inside!

Alone...

Slowly I turn around. The room is dark, not black, but dark. You wouldn't see the difference, but me, I live it.

I turn my face to the exit, which is closed, with Violette beyond it, ceaselessly bumping into the elevator doors; this image haunts me. It's my fault if she's there, in such a bad state. I hope that the room releases me quickly or that someone will come.

What are the chances of somebody wandering around here in the middle of the night? I prefer to drive this idea out of my head otherwise I'll go crazy!

Nobody is going to come...

Nobody...

With a stroke of my hand, I wipe away the tears flowing from my eyes. I have to pull myself together and understand what more the room wants! I wheel into the center of the room, the blackness envelops me... I'm cold. I stop and stare at the wall like a madman, like the madman I've become. What folly to believe that things could work out for me, I'm definitely condemned to be in this chair, and I believed it might be otherwise, and I brought Violette into this madness!

By dint of staring at the wall, I see things, I hope for things, but nothing comes independently into my imagination. The wall stays blank, sterile. Why didn't it let me go out if nothing is going to happen?

I have the feeling of being here for hours, in this nothingness, this void. Not a sound from outside, everything here is sealed. I'm not even looking at the wall any more, I'm just waiting to be released. Then, just as I've no hope left, a bright spot appears. Not on the wall, no! But right in the middle of the room a few inches from me. I hold out my hand, but I can't touch it, despite it being so close. The outlines of this spot begin to vibrate, to shimmer. It expands slowly. It isn't very bright, it looks like a cloud of smoke, opaque and odorless. I widen my eyes in an attempt to distinguish something inside, as it grows bigger and bigger. Soon, in front of me, the point has become as large as me. I step back a little, because now I'm afraid of it swallowing me up. I'm afraid of losing myself, of falling into it. I feel a sense of vertigo overcoming me, so I look away, but nothing catches my eye, there's just this gaping hole in front of me. Moving like quicksand, it gradually fills the space of the room. I've nothing to hold on to except my chair, my fingers are clutching my wheels. I feel that my knuckles could be pulled out of my fingers, the pressure is that strong. I have sore hands, so I let go a little and I massage them, they're icy cold.

Suddenly, like a big mouth; the void swallows me up... I spin round, clinging tightly back onto what's left of my reality: my chair! But for how long? I can't hold on any more, I let go... I find myself standing up! Standing on white ground. Everything has stopped turning, I stamp my foot on the ground; it's solid. However I don't dare to move, I don't quite comprehend it. I look at my watch, what a surprise to realize that I've only been here for 5 minutes, yet it seemed such a long time. And for Violette, what's happening for her out there? I hear footsteps... They come up close, but I can't see anything.

"Hello, Louie" says a disembodied voice.

I'm looking all around, there's no one here, but that voice... and this breath! I know this isn't mine!

"Who are you?"

A loud and insane laugh rings out, but I don't let it faze me.

"My question isn't funny!"

"Indeed! Who do you think I am?"

"I haven't the slightest idea."

A current of air passes through me, it's very close to me. I can feel a chill running down my spine.

"It's a pity," whispers the invisible voice.

I turn around with a jump.

"How's Violette?"

"She's very well, so stop worrying about her!"

"And you stop playing with me."

"You really think this is a game, Louie?"

"I don't know anymore what to think," I say, finally.

I hear a cracking sound behind me, I turn around. A tree appears, it's so very real. Then another and another, and soon I find myself in a forest! I'm cold... again. An owl is hooting, but I can't see it; there are only trees, ferns and a carpet of leaves: an autumnal carpet.

"Who are you? Why do you make me endure this?"

"Endure, is that the right word?"

"Yes."

"No! Living is more correct. Why am I making you live through this? Because I believe in your potential."

"My potential..."

"Are you so cold?"

I'm shivering.

"Yes..."

In one second, the forest changes into a beach, trees become pebbles, I hear a seagull that I can't see, like the owl. The sun warms me.

"Thanks!"

"Indeed, it's not much. What do you want most in your little life, Louie?"

Its tone is mocking. It's mocking my physical condition, my disability. I don't answer, I won't yield to its attack. Of what potential did the voice speak?

"Your potential to believe the impossible, to convince others."

There, he's reading in my thoughts now!

"But?"

I must get out of this evil room.

"You can only get out when my desire will be to let you out. All is not as simple as your simple wish. Answer my question."

"You know the answer very well. Why are you playing?"

I insist.

"I want to hear you say it."

"Ask a deaf man what he desires the most in the world!"

"You're not deaf."

"Luckily for you; it would be difficult to communicate, because I can't see you."

"You're not hearing me, it's an illusion."

"I hear you very well."

"In your head yes! But here you only hear the seagulls on the beach without sea."

I hadn't noticed that there wasn't just a beach or rather an expanse. I'd mistakenly thought it was the sea. The voice in my head was right.

"I would like to regain the use of my legs and everything that hasn't worked since that stupid accident!"

"There you are, that's good."

"Glad to make you happy," I say, in conclusion, tired of this dialogue.

Everything is fading away, I now find myself in the heart of a volcano, and God how it's hot. I'm sweating large beads.

"See you soon, Louie."

Then nothing more... Nothing other than the room which has reverted to a normal laundry again, here in the hospital. I'm once again sitting in my chair; I head towards the door, which opens normally. I go out, I look all around and there is nobody there. I'm not even sure where I am any more. I wheel myself several yards towards the elevators, far away from that room. I'm frightened now, but first of all I have to find Violette!

I wheel myself along like crazy, but to where? Who? What?...

"Where are you going like that, Louie?" A familiar voice yells from behind me.

I turn around to face Henri.

"I'm looking for Violette!"

He catches me up too easily, and stops my chair.

"It's time to dine, you'll see her later or tomorrow. I don't know if she's even still here at this hour."

He starts pushing me towards the refectory... against my will.

"I have to see her now."

I almost shout, putting on the brakes. I must still be the master of my wheelchair!

He places himself in front of me, very discontentedly.

"What's the matter?"

"I just want to know how she's doing."

He leans over to me, frowning.

"Why wouldn't she feel well?"

His question is sincere, he doesn't understand my attitude. But I say nothing, I don't want to join Christian. I don't want to be his cell-mate.

"Have you seen her this afternoon?"

"Did you fall in love with your psychiatrist?"

I sense that I'm going to get bogged down with this.

"Forget it. Let's go to dinner!"

"Tztzttztz, you've said too much, yet also not quite enough. Come on! Louie, tell me."

I don't know how to get out of the impasse in which I've got myself stuck. I already had, in the past, the annoying habit of finding myself in impossible situations, but I used to have the opportunity to flee, which isn't the case today. In a room or elsewhere, when someone catches me, I'm cornered.

But without knowing why, Henri now ceases to stare at me, he gets up and pushes me towards the refectory. He hums merrily behind me, and I shut myself up. If something serious had happened to Violette, he would tell me. How was it possible that she left that room intact? She was struck by lightning in that room! Yes, but what happened when she was outside? Apparently nothing... But I wanted to see her to be sure. Because, at the moment, the only image of her which remained in my mind, was of her lifeless body in her chair, bumping into the elevator doors before the room trapped me again. A very bad image to stick in my brain and in my vision.

Arriving at the refectory, we come across the director, and I grab him by his arm. What an idiot! Surprised, he looks at me.

"Yes?"

"Where's Violette?"

"At home, I presume," he says, staring hard at me.

"Have you seen her this afternoon?"

"Of course!"

"Are you sure?"

I need to know. He brings his gaze from me over to Henri, quizzically.

"Absolutely certain," he says, in conclusion, after a few seconds.

He puts his hand on my shoulder with a sigh, and continues on his way. He knows that his residents can be strange sometimes, he's used to it. Henri takes me over to my table. I can sense the director's eyes on me. I have to make myself very small, even smaller than I already am. Henri whispers in my ear while he adjusts my chair.

"You need to calm down, she's well."

"How can you be certain?"

He brings my plate and grabs the mayonnaise jar. He serves me more than necessary, and speaks to me.

"We had our meeting this afternoon. She left at 5pm like the rest of us, tired of course; but she was fine."

I smile stupidly at him, my mind going a hundred miles an hour. By then, it would've been a long time since she'd come out of that room. I'm reassured, but not convinced.

"Thanks..."

My heartbeat finally will be able to rest, not to pause, but just to slow down: to move to a slower pace. She's well, nothing is understandable, but she's safe and sound. I don't care about the rest. I can finally throw myself at my French-fries!

After the meal, upon my request, my favorite caregiver brings me back to my room. I need peace, and the common-rooms are not conducive to peace.

I need to understand what happened to me in the room while I was alone there.

I need to understand why Violette is well.

I need to know to whom I spoke...

Sleep isn't likely to offer me company tonight.

Yet... it's into a deep sleep that I fall, heavily. Something comes to me... in full consciousness. I'm not dreaming, I'm living through it.

I'm standing in a room. The walls are decorated tastefully, there's a black leather couch in front of a glass coffee table. All of that is facing a television. Amounting to a lounge quite commonplace, in a house in the city center judging by what I can see through the window. It's on the ground floor, this place could be my own. It's in my image; simple, clean and functional. Everything seems normal, except for me, who is standing. It's snowing.

I toss and turn, this room seems familiar to me, yet I've never set foot or even wheels here. I know that I'm far away from the room with the blue door, I'm lying in my bed. I know it, I feel it. I don't have the feeling that I'm dreaming, but it can't be anything else, can it?

Someone knocks on the door, making me jump! I approach it slowly and look through the peephole. I don't know this face; my curiosity prevails and I open the door.

"Hi, can I help you?"

Facing me, the man smiles, as if I'd said something funny. He takes a step forward, I block his way by placing my hand on the door jamb.

"Please Louie, stop being childish and let me in."

"Do we know each other?"

"Of course, otherwise why would I be here?"

This can't be wrong; he doesn't have a briefcase. So that says I know him. I lower my arm again, move away from the door and invite him in, with a wave of my hand. I close the door again behind him and watch him head into the lounge. He sits down on my couch, at least I think that it's mine. He seems to be at ease. His face I don't recognize, but his voice isn't unfamiliar. I don't want to believe my first thought. I go over to join him slowly, giving me a bit of time to think. However, I decide to venture into dangerous territory for me:

"Why did Christian hear several voices?"

"Well," he says...

Just that: a 'well'!

"Well what?"

"You're starting to make some good associations. I'm delighted about it."

"Why?"

"This says that you're starting to believe more than just what you see."

He gives me a headache with his riddles.

"And?"

"Your mind is opening up to me. I'm becoming real to you."

"You're not real?"

"That depends for whom; even if the whole world believes in my existence, nobody really wants to believe it."

"Why?"

"Don't you have any other questions than just "*why*"?"

"And you, don't you have any other answers than just your riddles?"

I'm in a dream, I repeat this phrase to myself in my mind, while his red eyes stare at me. I don't look down with mine, I'm not afraid of anything, I'm dreaming! But the more he looks at me, the more he penetrates my soul and it becomes unbearable for me. I collapse on the floor, exhausted. He stands up, and paces up and down as I'm lying on the floor. On what is perhaps my carpet.

"Christian heard several voices, because he didn't listen to my own."

"Did he defy you?" I'm at pains to say.

"In a way, yes. He dared to defy me."

I feel my body rise up and gently place itself on my couch. But I'm dreaming, so I couldn't care less what happens to me. Anything can happen in a dream or a nightmare. I like to believe that, at this precise moment. Then, he leans over me. He's not touching me, he's just right there above me, his face so close to mine.

"What do you want from me?"

"You!"

"Uh... I'm not that way inclined!" I say, lifting myself up a little.

He bursts into a loud laughter, so loud that it fills my head to almost exploding. I close my eyes and hold my

head, gripping my hands around it like a vice... Let it
stop!

So slowly, calm returns. I open one eye, and then the other, surprised to no longer find myself in my living room!

Instead of two red eyes staring at me, I'm plunged into the blue ocean of those of Violette. She is really there for sure. I'm in my room once again; I hadn't left my bed for a single moment, but I'm back here in my reality. I sit up abruptly.

"How are you, Violette?"

She's looking at me, visibly surprised by my question.

"Why wouldn't I be well?" she asks, as she puts her hand on my forehead.

Do I look sick?

"You'd been struck by lightning..."

"Pardon?"

"In the room... Don't you remember?"

"We didn't find that damn room. You've said it yourself, that it doesn't show itself in the daytime. Besides, this is why I'm here."

She finishes her sentence in a whisper.

She doesn't remember anything. She's come to look for me to go back there!

"You'd like to go back there now?"

"Well, it's night. Isn't this the best time for it? What happened to you, Louie?"

I stare at her not knowing what to do or what to say. I can't tell her about my dream, nor about this afternoon in the room.

"Let's go..."

I automatically press the bell; I need someone who can put me into my wheelchair, it's not as if I'm doing what I want when I want, at least not here and now. It's a cruel life! The night man arrives, he's no longer surprised by my request. Violette and I, we're going for a wander. He doesn't pay it any more attention.

Once again, here I am, wheeling myself behind Violette.

I'm having a hard time getting rid of that vision of her head banging against the elevator, her head jolting with every impact on the metal. But she doesn't remember that, so where is the problem? All's well, but I know very well that I didn't dream it!

She waits in front of the button, I look at her with a smile. Does she wonder whether something isn't normal? Why is it just me who can foresee it? We rush into the square and cold compartment. Violette is still cheerful about the idea of going back into the room with the blue door, I'm dreading that it will make us suffer.

"You look worried, Louie. Is everything okay?"

"Yes, I'm still a little sleepy, that's all," I lie to her...

Over these last few days, Violette and I have become closer. We haven't talked about it, it happened naturally. It's absolutely forbidden for staff to get attached to patients. These patients who are so fragile that they may at any time freak out, give up and abandon the premises.

Me, I wouldn't leave. I'm not here to give in, I am tenacious. I yearn to ride on my highway, riding my Harley without assistance. So, give up: never! And now, a new perspective opens up to me. Although I still don't understand everything, I have this feeling that something might change for my benefit. Anyway, I firmly hope so.

The doors open onto the corridor of SS2, I'm following Violette closely, she's determined in her nocturnal search. The door shows itself almost immediately, which is positive: it doesn't make us "*run*" everywhere. It happily offers itself for our visit.

All this will have a price...

"Look, here it is," announces Violette, excitedly.

"Yes, and already open,"

I reply, in a tone that I hope seems cheerful. She turns towards me.

"After you!"

"No, no; ladies first."

"You're strange, Louie..."

"No, just still a little in my dreams, don't worry. I should've had a coffee."

"Too late now," she says, as she enters the doorway.

I try to look inside, but as usual, just that blinding light leaks out from the room. What will it have in store for us? Will my fears influence it in any way? I hope not, otherwise we'll be in for a real hell. I put my hands on the wheels and propel myself inside; as soon as I pass the doorway, it closes behind me. This same little noise keeps me from having to turn my head around.

I'm sweating like a madman.

In the bright whiteness, a black grand piano appears, a remarkable contrast. It would seem that it's nothing too threatening. Then the room plunges us into a total darkness, when, accompanied by a click, the beam of a spotlight lands on the piano, lacking only the pianist. I don't play piano!

Violette and I, we look at each other, questioningly. She starts to grimace, as her shadow detaches from her. Movements become painful; this separation brings us more and more suffering. She doesn't walk to the piano, but flies instead! That's new... Delicately, the graceful shape sits on the stool, the fabric gently resting on its figure. Its hands are placed on its knees.

"You know how to play the piano?"

I ask her, in a whisper, knowing that the room doesn't like to be disturbed.

"I learned when I was young, but..."

After a pause, she continues.

"I wasn't very good, so I gave up the idea of being a virtuoso."

A first note sounded in the room; timid, barely audible. 'She' places her second hand on the keyboard. I imagine the stress oozing at the idea of not being successful again. But this here is the room of all hopes! Gracefully, she caresses the keys. Almost one by one, are they taming her? A first one is struck in, followed by a second. I see 'her' place her feet on the pedals; the reflexes are returning. Violette, beside me, closes her eyes, letting inspiration pervade her. A sweet melody begins to fill the space, as I can feel by the tips of my feet that my own shadow wants to join in. Slowly, it extracts itself out of me, without too much pain, to go and sit where I didn't think it would: on the piano. Its head turns towards the keyboard, I can feel its eyes follow the nimble fingers of Violette's shadow. She shouldn't have had to give up the piano. Her fingers, so fine, are so beautiful traversing the path of the black and white keys. They know where to put themselves for the sound that comes out to be strong and harmonious. She shouldn't have had to give up the piano!

A fresh light breeze moves her hair; she is beautiful. I lose myself in the grace of the moment, my head is spinning...

Far, far away, I hear her screaming...
A scream which resounds without end, an echo writhing in pain. I look at the piano, anxiously. No one is playing it, yet the music still comes to my ears, interlaced with her screams of terror.

So, my gaze turns to Violette's chair; it's empty! How is this possible? Where did she go? Could the room have consumed her? I erase these completely absurd ideas from my mind. Here, this world is unreal.

The last time, nothing happened to her, and I'd almost made people worried by questioning them so hard. Worried about me, which is rather dangerous. But, I must admit my sanity is beginning to escape me. I'm lost... I don't understand it all and I'm horrified at not being the master of my actions or even of my thoughts. For my actions are now managed by others, well at least my movements are. Because there is a difference.

All this is becoming cruel, cruel to the point of no return if I'm not careful.

I don't have to yield to panic, nevertheless it's starting to overcome me, as Violette's voice fades away into nothingness. Where did her body go? I'm haunted by this. I jump off the piano and land on my two legs. A cry of pain escapes from my mouth, very real this one! The floor looks like a large cloud, I'm clinging to the piano; I don't want to disappear as well. I go over to the stool; it is indeed quite empty. Pausing for a moment, I try to understand and find an explanation.

I'm still curious about this room, but I'm torn by the urge to leave, to see if Violette is alright. Alas, I'm afraid I can't do that, however hard I yearn to. HE certainly won't let me go out. It's not in his disposition to do MY bidding. So I attempt to chase away Violette from my thoughts, and reassure myself once again: "She's alright!" And so, I decide to let this, Machiavellian room, be. So I sit myself down at the piano, without playing, and I wait.

The clouds turn grey now, becoming like the day of a tempest; the breeze changes into an icy blizzard, lashing my face and freezing my hands. I rub them vigorously to warm myself up. The piano is no longer black, but now white. The room is reversing the role of each thing; everything becomes the negative of its former positive. Even the piano keys are reversed! The most morbid thought that there could be, comes to mind: and if Violette would be brought back but now dead! This would make sense; unless that it's me who is dead! If it's a choice, I don't know if I would sacrifice myself.

I'm now in total darkness, and I still don't give in to that panic which knocks ceaselessly at the door of my soul. I breathe deeply as I'd been taught to do... before. The air oxygenates my brain; the deeper my breaths are, the more the air flows in, and the better I feel. If I had a plastic bag, I would have placed it over my mouth to calm my anxiety attack. When I was young, I was subject to this kind of condition, and the doctor who took care of me gave me this tip in case of an impending attack. It had to be nipped in the bud, so he said; never let it escalate otherwise the attack would gather momentum and not very much other than strong medication would stop it.

So I calm myself down, right now, here in this world which only exists for a few. My strategy seems to work, but now I'm cold… since now snow is falling.

A loud noise startled me and made my feet jump sharply from my little stool. Behind me, a flash of lightning split the black-grey sky. I look all around me; nothing to protect me, nowhere to shelter. Things become complicated; I breathe into my hands, my warm breath confirms that I am still alive, but for how long? A small cloud of warm breath issues from my mouth, it's cold, very cold. My feet start to ache. Nothing's improving, yet my host doesn't show himself. He remains silent, probably somewhere watching me die. Does this please him? Was this his purpose? I think about my bed, the warmth of my duvet. I like this vision of the world outside when I'm tucked up safely in my bed. I try to keep that thought in my mind. It does me good and allows me to fight against the elements which are now raging around me. I put my hands between my thighs to keep them a little warmer. I'm shivering; my whole body is trembling with cold. Stronger still, a sound makes me turn my head; the piano slowly slides sideways to eventually disappear beneath the cloud. No further noises permit me to establish whether or not it landed anywhere. A bottomless fall into an imaginary world, nevertheless so real.

"Louie... Louie; wake up!"

A reassuring voice pulls me back from the room, from my nightmare, from my torture! I slowly open my eyes upon Violette! But her face is blurred, or is it my eyes which need time to adjust. Then I'm surprised by a height detail: She's standing, bending down over me! Her face is still not quite distinct, as if her skin was moving, as if... something was swarming about beneath her skin.

An unreal and frightening vision!

I bring my hand up to her face because I want to make sure of it for myself. Instead of touching her soft skin, my fingers sink into a kind of treacle. I withdraw my hand in disgust. This isn't Violette who's standing above me!

"Come Louie, join me..."

"Who...?"

By way of a response, again that malign laughter resounds inside my head. I shake my head in the hope of escaping from this nightmare. Over a few seconds, the scenery fades away from my sight, and I'm still sitting in my wheelchair in the middle of this room, which is too white, too sanitized. Then, a second later, I can again see what might be Violette looking at me, but I know it's not her. That can't be her.

I'm in my bed, and I'm straightening myself up; after all, here... I'm able-bodied! And it works, as my mind takes over and I sit up. It, that thing, is a few yards away from me and is smiling. Its smile is hideous, its teeth look dirty, blackened by something. So, I look away from this false Violette, trying to win me over. My gaze falls on her hands though, yet those aren't her hands. She would never let them be so poorly kept. The outline of the nails is also black. Then suddenly, the most frightful thoughts invade my mind; perhaps what I could see here was indeed my Violette, but in an early state of decomposition! What if she was dead this time, and not quietly sleeping in her bed or in the room next to me in her wheelchair? What if...

I shake my head again, trying to chase away the terrible vision. Once again, this action allows me to glimpse where I really am, but this time I can't see Violette near me. She's disappeared. The room did take her away, but to where? All of these questions and concerns trigger the early stages of a migraine. Decidedly, this place makes me live through all the ills which nobody would want to feel. Anguish, pain, headache... my body tries to bear the unbearable... without really knowing why. At this point she comes and sits on the edge of my bed, I'm taken aback. Who would have thought that I could feel disgust for her. I pull the sheets back up to my face; a meagre protection against this thing, a useless protection. She's smiling again, one of those haggard smiles that scares children. I'm not panicking... my subconscious is helping me to hold on, but I must admit that she frightens me. She opens her mouth.

"Come Louie, join me... " she says, offering me her hand.

Her voice, usually so sweet, is raucous. A nauseating stench reaches my nostrils, I discreetly pull the sheet over my nose. I daren't confirm to myself my suspicions about this thing. I don't want to admit that I'm speaking with something dead.

"What did you do to Violette?"

"Ah! Violette, always Violette," it starts shouting, raising its body up, that which has assumed an approximate likeness to my friend.

I open my eyes widely. By all accounts, I annoyed it with my question. He or she is now walking up and down in front of me, making grand gestures with its arms. The sounds coming out of its mouth more resemble cries than words. I don't understand them, maybe it's another language. I have nowhere to run to. I'm at its mercy. After all, whether here or elsewhere, it would still be the same. But I decide not to let myself be beaten down by its cries or by my mind telling me to give up, and I jump out of bed with incredible ease; surprising even. I must stop underestimating myself! I'm safe, at least I think so, at the other side of the bed. A deafening noise rings out. It's so loud that I can't hear this creature shouting. My feeble protection is about to collapse; in one fell swoop, the floor opens up and the bed sinks into the void. Like with the piano earlier, the sound of its impact doesn't come to my ears; beneath my feet is just nothingness. This gives me a feeling of vertigo, and I look for something to hold onto.

Behind me is my window, or a replica of the one in my room, so I take a few steps back without turning round and I hold onto it. I must not turn my back to this Violette. My fingers are clenched onto the windowsill, it's hurting me. This makes me forget my head and everything else a little. I try to stay focused on my pain, watching the monster which now faces me.

It's nothing at all like my loved one; I watch her slacken her neck, her joints make a noise as she changes her form. Her hair turns black. She holds her hands out and spreads her fingers; each knuckle making a noise, a crack, as her fingers elongate. Her black nails make me think of a witch. I'm beginning to understand what it was that was standing in front of me before the start of this metamorphosis: this must be what had been superimposed onto Violette, I could now see both bodies at the same time.

I knew that Violette wouldn't be that unkempt!

I can't push the window open behind me, I can't flee, I can't wake up because I'm not asleep! I can only face the impossible. I crave Christian's padded room... I envy and understand his decision...

I'm frightened; very frightened, and I know that such an animal as this, which is unfolding before my eyes, can feel my fear.

And here... is the greatest of all dangers.

Never has this room seemed so real! I'm trying not to panic, which would incidentally be completely useless. But on the other hand, it would probably make me lapse into insanity. Madness as an escape might perhaps be a good option, since now my eyes were taking in the rest of my room. It was all just an illusion: Violette, my room, my bed... The only real things here are that thing and me, even if I am standing up; which would be completely impossible... at this stage anyway. Maybe in a few months' time, after a long rehabilitation, I could eventually hope to take a few steps. So there's no point in fleeing into madness, I have to face up to this because there is always hope.

I'm keeping my eyes on that creature. I'm reassuring myself by telling myself that while it's silent, I have nothing to fear. So I just observe it. The upper body is still vague, but the lower half presents a surreal sight, and I understand what I'm seeing. Its feet are huge and hairy. I can count six toes ending in black nails, far too long to be human. The sixth toe is bent, clawed, certainly to allow a better grip and a more stable footing. This resembles nothing which I could think of or imagine. Then, my eyes slowly trace the length of its similarly hairy calves. Its carmine-red skin is covered in darker fissures. Its skin is like leather, it seems thick and solid: invulnerable. Its muscular chest rises rhythmically. It lives, it breathes. I focus on this muscular mass, because I'm afraid to look at its face. Now I switch my gaze again to its hands... its nails are even longer than they were a few minutes earlier. One scratch would cut me in two. A bear wouldn't measure up in the face of this thing. At the moment when its transformation seems to be coming to an end, I can see, unfurling behind it, a tail; long, and devoid of the slightest hair. Its color is very much darker than the rest of its body. This nightmare will have no ending, I know that now. All of this is real, very real... It's here, right in front of me. Now that I'm accepting the idea of it, I stare defiantly at it. Its large red eyes are staring at me while it grimaces one last time. It spreads its arms open wide, displaying all its splendor, and I notice that in pride of place on its head are two horns!

This thing has a name, I know it, I'm familiar with it, but I will not speak it. That would be asking for it!

It's large, very large; too large to engage in any battle. It stands a little hunched over, as if it's used to being in places which are too low, too small. Confined spaces which are designed for other creatures: humans. Just as my eyes are finishing their tour around this thing, I feel a hot breath coming to land on my face, and a strong, serious voice speaks up:

"What have you decided, Louie?"

It's showing itself out in the open, because its patience is at an end. That's what I imagine. I tell myself also that either I get out of here feet first, or remain on my two inferior legs. The decision is mine. I understand what I have to gain, but what does it want from me?

"You have to decide, here and now!"

I hesitate to speak for a moment. I don't want to unleash this being on myself. I've had my fair share of suffering.

"What do you have to gain from this?" I ask.

I'm reckless, but nothing ventured, nothing gained and I have nothing more to lose... at all.

"You... of course"

I try as hard as I can to withstand its gaze, but its red eyes are deep and burn my soul.

"But what can I bring for you?"

"Think about it, Louie..."

It's not threatening, which is strange at any rate.

I'm thinking hard, but I don't understand.

"You want my life?"

"I want all of you; your life, your breath, your essence... your physical form..."

It's scaring me, here and now; I'm dying of fright, but I'm trying not to show it. And I hope it won't feel it too.

"... And your loyalty. You're going to belong to me whether you like it or not. You came to me, Louie. You alone have sealed your fate. I've only responded to your call."

I'm frowning, trying to take in what it's now saying. I remain mute and it continues its well-rehearsed speech; I'm not the first and neither will I be the last.

"You will be devoted to me, body and soul… in return I'll let you play with the destiny of others."

"That's to say?"

It takes a step towards me, and I can feel the vibrations of its power through the soil.

"Don't disappoint me! Stop playing the fool!"

The closer it approaches me, the hotter I feel. My fingers sink into the windowsill as if it were made of clay, which isn't the case. I'm falling against the window… it's only a few inches from my face now. Its breath is foul, I turn my head away in disgust.

"So, Louie?"

"Do I have a choice?"

It stands up.

I slowly raise my eyes to this mountain made of muscle, of hatred and of power. Its head touches the ceiling of my room, exploding it; revealing the sky, which is fiery red. I'm hot, more and more hot. My body boils. Sweat drips from my whole being, reminding me that I'm still alive.

"Hahahahhaha… No! Of course not. You've come to the point of no return. I'm standing here in front of you… Me!"

It leans over again towards me.

"Your answer, now!" It says, while its tail is loudly whipping the floor, betraying its impatience.

"I haven't understood everything… but I accept," I finally say, with my eyes cast down.

I've barely finished these words, when it put its huge, hairy hand on my head. Sounds resound inside me, words which I don't understand.

"Θα έρθει σε μένα, θα δώσετε στον εαυτό σας ν
α μου ... την αφοσίωσή σας θα ζήσουν μέχρι και τ
ην προστασία μου ... μπαίνει σφαίρα μου από πυρκ
αγιά ... είναι δική μου ... τώρα![1] »

I feel my essence escaping; my breath becomes short
and I collapse on the floor...

---

[1] "To me you come, to me you give yourself... Your commitment will be at the level of
my protection... Enter my realm of fire... Be mine... Now!

Hello, my name is Louie, you know me... you remember this highway, the truck coming up behind me... then there was all that time and that suffering... this extraordinary discovery and... all things considered, I had said **yes** to this thing.

Today I find myself back on my vehicle, riding towards Namur. In my mirror, there's a truck. It's travelling very fast, much too fast; so I accelerate... I won't let him catch up with me, not this time. I take a big lead for myself, and while I'm riding I turn to look at him.

I fear nothing.

I see it, large and about to crash into me.

I raise my hand and the very second afterwards, the truck's grille buckles, stopped in its tracks. The trailer doesn't stop and crashes into the cab which is now immobile. There is an enormous racket as the metal crumples. I look closely at the man's face; he's surprised, but also ready to confront death. This inevitable death, because for him there will be no second chance. The space between him, the windscreen and the trailer is shrinking.

He has no escape. His look shows that he has understood; perhaps he's praying.

The windscreen explodes under the pressure of the body and the rest of the truck. It, which was once so big, is now reduced into a few yards. Things are as they should be. The pieces of windscreen are dripping with blood and bruised flesh, the body is no more, it has merged with the truck; they are now one.

Behind it, the cars brake, honk their horns, and swerve to a halt. People come running, but it's too late. Fate has caught up with the driver. There is nothing left of him now except for his truck as a tomb.

With another gesture of his hand, Louie sets the whole pile ablaze; on his face a smirk of revenge. His past is going up in smoke, now he can continue his journey in complete peace of mind.

Now, he's perhaps invisible... but he's invincible! Now, he's big and strong so all the trucks in the world should beware.

Violette entered Louie's room. It'd been several days now since he'd disappeared. She was worried, because she liked Louie very much, but also because of that room. She began searching in the room, looking for a few clues here. She found a notebook. She wheeled over to the window facing the garden, and placed it on her lap, then she opened it. The notebook was witness to what had happened in the room, she read it and discovered that her feelings were shared. She raised her head towards the outside world, disappointed.

Disappointed that he hadn't said anything to her, even though some signs had let her catch a glimpse of that still shy feeling.

She read all morning long, and she was frightened because the things in the room had been very different for him. Around 3pm, after she'd missed lunch, she finally came to the last page. On it were these words:

"I'll come back to find you, Violette..."

She closed the book with a smile, she trusted him; although after reading this, perhaps he wouldn't be the same.

She just wanted to be able to walk with him...

No matter what the price would be!

The end.

Find all of my publications on my website:

https://sylvieginestet.wordpress.com/

Join me on Facebook:
https://www.facebook.com/SylvieGinestetAuteur
www.facebook.com/SylvieGinestetTheQuest

Follow me on Twitter:
https://twitter.com/sylvieginestet

N° d'impression : 343798